Christmas on the Street

The Secret of the Second Basement

For Jordan Elizabeth Cooper

3558 S. Jefferson Avenue, St. Louis, MO 63118-3968
Manufactured in the United States of America.

Library of Congress Cataloging in Publication Data

Greene, Carol.
Christmas on the street.

Summary: Christmas looms bleakly for a group of street people living in a church subbasement, until a little girl comes to join them.
1. Children's stories, American. [1. Christmas—Fiction. 2. Puppets—Fiction] I. Boyanchek, Dave, ill. II. Title.
PZ7.G82845Ch 1984 [Fic] 84-15523
ISBN 0-570-04107-4

1 2 3 4 5 6 7 8 9 10 DB 93 92 91 90 89 88 87 86 85 84

Christmas on the Street

The Secret of the Second Basement

by Carol Greene

featuring
Dave Pavelonis' Peppercorn Puppets

photographed by
Herb Halpern and David Boyanchek

Cover photography: Val Gelineau

Publishing House
St. Louis

In an old part of the city, where the buildings look like ice cream sundaes frozen in stone, stands the Church of the Good Shepherd. It, too, is old, and in its tower hangs an old bell whose deep voice calls the faithful to worship each Sunday. But during the other six days of the week, the bell is silent and so, for the most part, is the rest of the church.

Hardly anyone ever went down into the basement of the church, except the janitor to check the furnace now and then, and even he never noticed the door in the back corner. But there was a door, tucked away behind boxes of old hymnals, and behind that door was a flight of stairs leading down to yet another basement. And in that second basement, deep underground, lived a family of street people.

Isaiah Bond was thinking about that family—*his* family—as he hurried back to the church late one December afternoon. It had been his turn to scout the trash containers in the park today, and he hadn't had much luck: two brown lunch bags with a few scraps in each and a half-empty box of stale popcorn.

I hope the others did better, he thought. *Otherwise it's going to be a sad supper. Boy, wouldn't it be great if I opened a trash can someday and found a whole roast turkey inside? Or a chocolate cake just dripping with frosting? Even some vegetables would be nice for a change.*

From this delicious daydream he slipped into another—what he'd give his family for Christmas if he had any money.

I'd get the Professor a book, he thought. *A book of essays by Ralph Waldo Emerson. The Professor's always spouting stuff from old Emerson. And I'd get Mrs. MacTuggle some warm, fuzzy bedroom slippers to wear when her feet are killing her.*

Of course, if I had a lot *of money, I'd get the three of us a house. Just a little house somewhere, where we could all live together like real people. Boy, would* that *be great!*

Isaiah was so lost in his daydreams that before he knew it, he was around the back of the church and halfway down the outside stairs that led to the first basement. He didn't even notice the bundle of rags at the bottom of the stairwell—at least not until he stepped on it.

"YOWRRRR!" A streak of gray exploded from the bundle and rocketed up the stairs.

"Great jumping fish feet!" Isaiah nearly leaped out of his tennis shoes.

Then the bundle of rags began to move and from it came a long, high wail. "Gaaaabriel!"

"Hush!" Isaiah didn't know what was in that bundle, but he knew he had to shut it up—fast. What if someone heard the noise and came back here to investigate? What if they found out about the second basement and the people living there? That was a secret that *had* to be kept. Quickly Isaiah reached out toward the rags.

"Don't touch me!" With a shudder the bundle scooted away from him and into a corner. Then, very slowly, it stood up.

"You're a little girl!" gasped Isaiah.

The rags, he now saw, were a coat, at least four sizes too big for the child who was wearing it. He couldn't see her hands or feet at all. But poking out of the top of the coat was an extremely dirty little face surrounded by a mop of spiky brown hair.

"I'm Nanny Feather," she snapped. "And don't you touch me."

Why, she's scared to death, thought Isaiah.

"I'm not going to touch you, Nanny Feather," he said gently. "I'll tell you what. Why don't you just sit down here on the steps and I'll go find Gabriel. He's your cat, isn't he?"

Nanny Feather nodded, but she didn't move from her corner.

"Okay," said Isaiah. "Stay there if you like. I'll be right back."

Fortunately, Gabriel hadn't gone far. Isaiah found him crouched beneath a bush in the yard.

"Pretty kitty. Hey, pretty kitty," he sweet-talked. Then he lunged and grabbed the cat.

"PURRRR!" Just like that, Gabriel went limp as a dishrag.

Isaiah carried him back to the stairwell. Nanny Feather was sitting down now. She was also trembling all over.

"What's the matter?" he asked.

She glared at him. "I'm cold, that's what's the matter. Give me Gabriel. And don't touch me!"

"I *said* I wouldn't touch you." Isaiah dumped the cat in her lap. Then he tried to decide what to do next.

"Um—would you like me to take you home?" he asked. "I mean, it's getting pretty late for a little kid to be out on her own."

"Haven't got a home," she mumbled.

"Aw, come on—" began Isaiah.

"I said I haven't got a home!" she yelled. "I—I—" She was silent for a few moments, as if she were seeing pictures and hearing sounds that no one else could see or hear. Then, suddenly, she screamed. "DON'T TOUCH ME!"

"Okay, little girl," soothed Isaiah. "It's okay." He had heard about abused children, and he had a feeling he was looking at one now.

What'll I do next? he wondered. *I can't leave her out here. But do I dare take her inside? What if she makes a lot of noise? What if she does something to get us all thrown out?*

But even as he asked himself these questions, Isaiah knew that the answers didn't matter. He had to take a chance.

"Come on, Nanny Feather," he said. "We're going inside. You have to get warm."

Nanny Feather didn't say anything as he used the key the Professor had given him to unlock the door. But she followed him in, Gabriel clutched tightly in her arms. Silently Isaiah led her to the door behind the hymnals and down the steps.

Mrs. MacTuggle was cooking something on the hotplate and the Professor was bent over a newspaper at the table. But they both turned around when Isaiah cleared his throat.

"Er—I've brough a guest, everybody. Her name's Nanny Feather. Nanny, this is the Professor and Mrs. MacTuggle."

Nanny Feather stepped out of the shadows behind him. "Wow, what a dump!" she said.

Isaiah whirled around. "It is *not* a dump! It's a great place to live compared to what lots of street people have. Why, how'd you like to sleep under a highway overpass? Or—"

"Isaiah Bond, you hush!" scolded Mrs. MacTuggle. "Where are your manners, I'd like to know? Look at this poor little thing, half-frozen. It's tea she needs—a nice hot cup of tea with plenty of sugar."

"Don't touch her," warned Isaiah as Mrs. MacTuggle bustled over. "She doesn't like anyone to touch her."

"Well, that's all right too. You come over here with me, Nanny Feather, and warm your hands at the hotplate while I put some water on."

"Yes, ma'am. Thank you, ma'am."

Hmf, thought Isaiah. *All of a sudden now she sounds like a sweet-tongued little angel.* He went over and sat down by the Professor.

"I didn't get much," he said, dumping his haul on the table.

"That's all right," said the Professor. "Mrs. M. came up with a soupbone."

"Hey, Professor." Isaiah lowered his voice to a whisper and pointed at Nanny Feather. "Do you think maybe she's crazy? I mean, she really does have a thing about people touching her. I think maybe she was abused or something."

He told the Professor how he'd found Nanny Feather and Gabriel.

"'A moody child and wildly wise,'" said the Professor. "That's Emerson. No, Isaiah, I don't think she's any crazier than the rest of us. Just coping with a bad time the best she knows how. You were right to bring her in."

Isaiah sighed. "That's a relief."

Before long, Mrs. MacTuggle had a cup of tea down Nanny Feather and was dishing up bowls of steaming soup.

"I took that bone right away from a big dog," she said proudly. "He was too fat for his own good anyway. Don't worry, Nanny Feather," she added. "I washed it."

But Nanny Feather didn't look at all worried, thought Isaiah. She still had that good little angel look about her. And she bowed her head along with everyone else when the Professor said grace.

"Thank You, Father, for Your many gifts," he prayed, "and especially for Nanny Feather and the soupbone. Bless us and keep us always mindful of the needs of others. Amen."

As they ate, Isaiah felt a warm glow spreading through him—and it wasn't just the soup. He felt good, good about his home and his family. Look at how they'd taken Nanny Feather in—just like that, without any questions. Of course that was how they'd taken him in too on that day long ago when his uncle had shoved him out of the car and told him to get lost. They were good folks all right, the Professor and Mrs. M. And Nanny Feather was looking better already.

After they'd finished eating, though, she stood up and wrapped her coat around her again.

"Thank you very much," she said politely. "I guess Gabriel and I had better be going now."

"Going?" said Isaiah. "Going where?"

"Well—" began Nanny Feather.

"You can stay here, if you like, Nanny Feather," said the Professor. "You can be part of our family, you and Gabriel both."

"But I'm not related," said Nanny Feather.

"So what?" said Isaiah. "Neither am I—really. Mrs. MacTuggle says we're all God's children. That's relation enough for us."

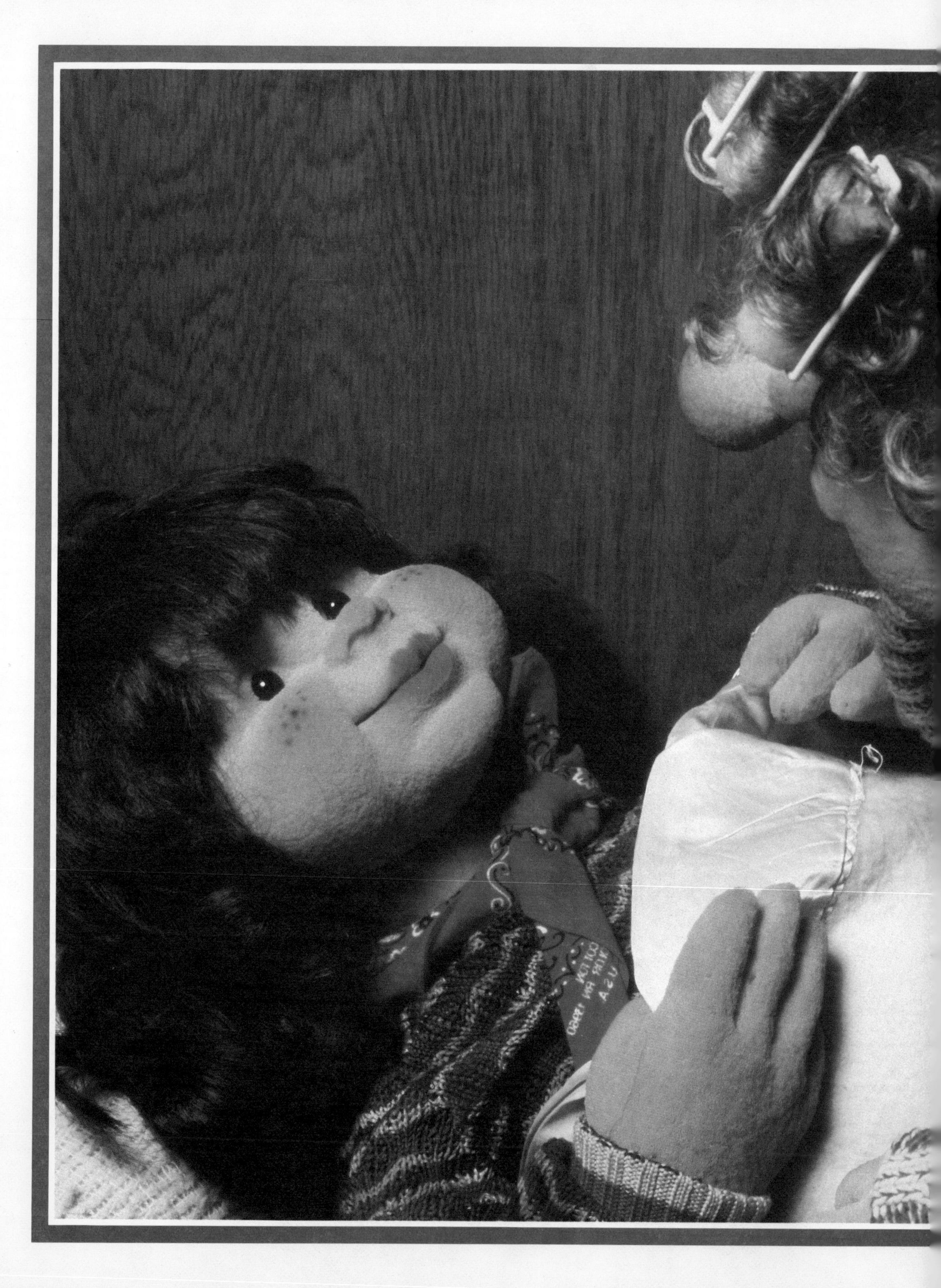

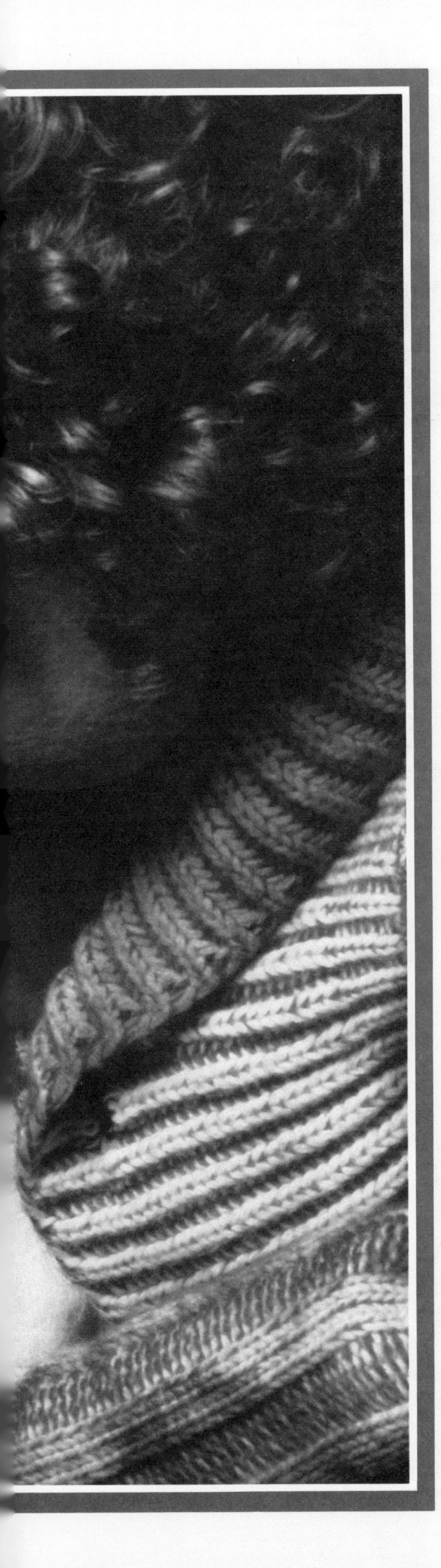

"Okay." Nanny Feather sat down and opened her coat again. "But you've all got to promise not to touch me. I break when people touch me. You can pet Gabriel, though. He likes it."

"Fine," said the Professor softly. "We'll pet Gabriel."

The second basement was filled with old pews and other forgotten church furnishings, so Mrs. MacTuggle had no trouble making up one more bed. From his own pew-bed, Isaiah watched as she threw a heavy cloth of some sort over Nanny Feather. She was very careful not to touch the little girl.

"Ma'am?" asked Nanny Feather as Gabriel settled himself in a purring ball on top of her. "Ma'am, you don't happen to have a doll down here, do you?"

Mrs. MacTuggle shook her head. "Why, no, child. I don't believe we do. Do you want a doll?"

Nanny Feather snuggled down. "Well, sort of. But that's okay. G'night."

The next morning the Professor greeted everyone with a new idea. Pickings, he said, were pretty slim in the trash cans this time of year. So why didn't they try something else for a while? Why not sing Christmas carols on the street corners?

"Folks would probably give us something if we did," he concluded, "and we could use the money to buy food."

"Great idea!" said Isaiah.

"Everyone likes to hear Christmas carols," added Mrs. MacTuggle.

"I can't sing," said Nanny Feather, looking sad. "Somebody once said my voice sounds like a rusty razor blade."

COLOMBO'S
SOUTH
GRAND
BARBER

"Doesn't matter," said the Professor. "Everyone can sing Christmas carols. Even rusty razor blades."

"Really?" said Nanny Feather.

"Really," said the Professor.

An hour later they found themselves on a busy street corner. The Professor held a tin cup for the money. Mrs. MacTuggle had her shopping bag for the food. Isaiah gripped a real tambourine he'd found in the second basement. And Nanny Feather pranced around in her big coat. Even Gabriel sat beside them, purring.

"All right," said the Professor. "Let's start with 'O Little Town.' Ready? One, two, three!"

"O little town of Bethlehem,
How still we see thee lie!
Above thy deep and dreamless sleep
The silent stars go by—"

They got that far and stopped. Around them horns blew and motors roared. Shoppers rushed past, their eyes glued to the ground. No one paid the least bit of attention to the carolers.

"Maybe city folks don't want to hear a song about a little town," suggested Nanny Feather.

"Nonsense!" said Mrs. MacTuggle. "Anyway, if *they* won't listen, we'll sing it for the Lord. Once more! One, two, three!"

"O little town of Bethlehem,
How still we see thee lie!
Above thy deep and dreamless sleep
The silent stars go by;
Yet in thy dark streets shineth
The everlasting Light;
The hopes and fears of all the years
Are met in thee tonight."

Then Isaiah heard it, the ching of a coin dropping into the Professor's cup. And another—and another. Grinning from ear to ear, he shook his tambourine even harder and went on singing.

"How silently, how silently,
The wondrous gift is giv'n!
So God imparts to human hearts
The blessings of His heav'n.
No ear may hear His coming,
But in this world of sin,
Where meek souls will receive Him, still
The dear Christ enters in."

He didn't even know he'd been singing a solo until people began to clap and an old gentleman patted his shoulder and said, "Fine voice, young man!" Then Isaiah beamed.

Later, on their way home, they stopped by a supermarket and Mrs. MacTuggle bought stew meat, potatoes, vegetables, milk, and—lo and behold!—chocolate cupcakes.

"Tonight," she said, "we are going to *eat!*"

And eat they did. Isaiah wasn't sure he'd ever be able to move again as he popped the last crumb of cupcake into his mouth.

"Why don't you take Nanny Feather upstairs and show her the church?" suggested the Professor. "You look as if you could use some exercise."

"Okay," agreed Isaiah.

"Isaiah?" said Nanny Feather when they'd reached the first basement. "Who are the Professor and Mrs. MacTuggle?"

"What do you mean, who are they?" said Isaiah. "They're my family. Your family too, now."

"I *know* that. But who are they otherwise? Who were they before—before they came here?"

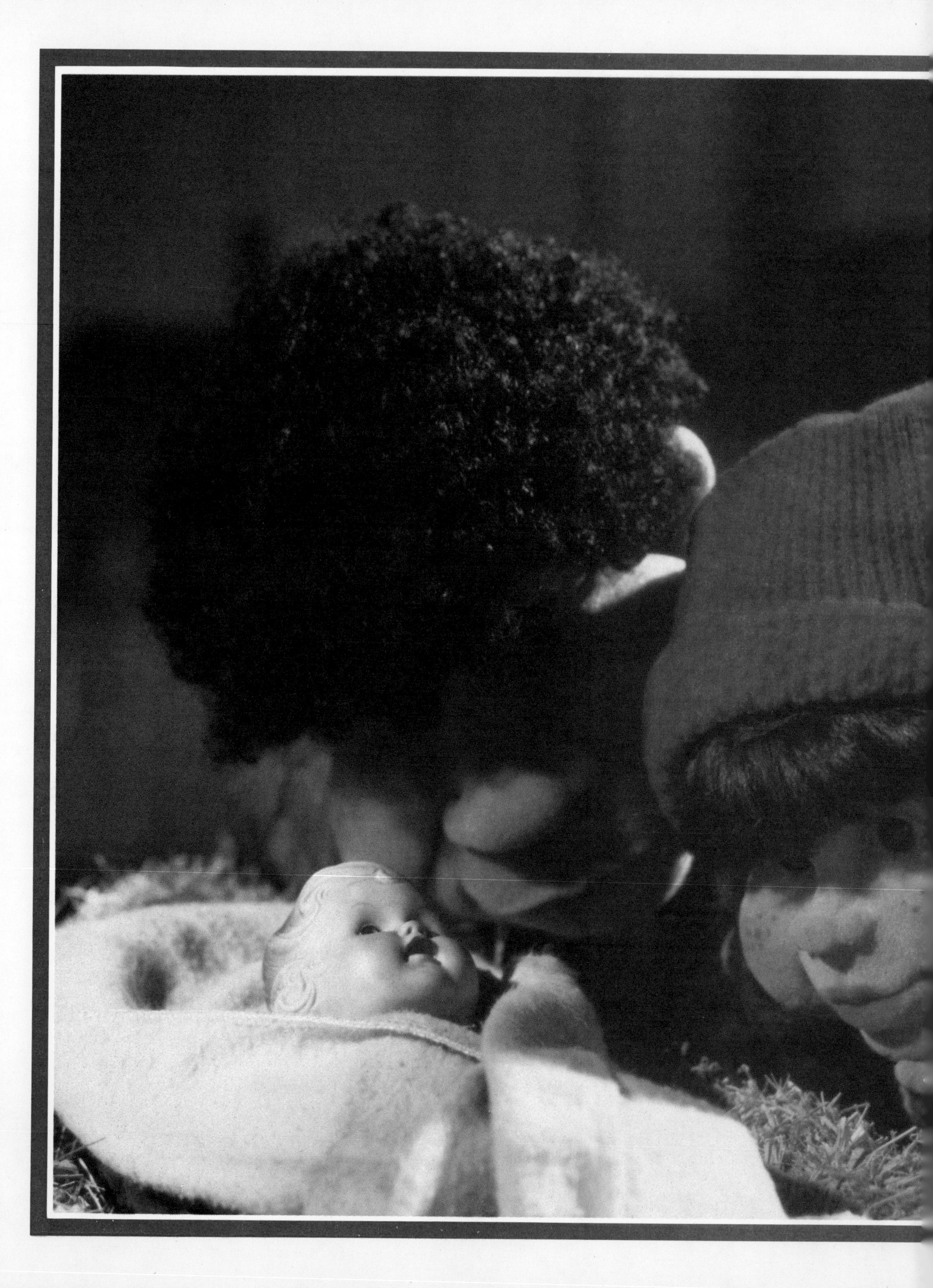

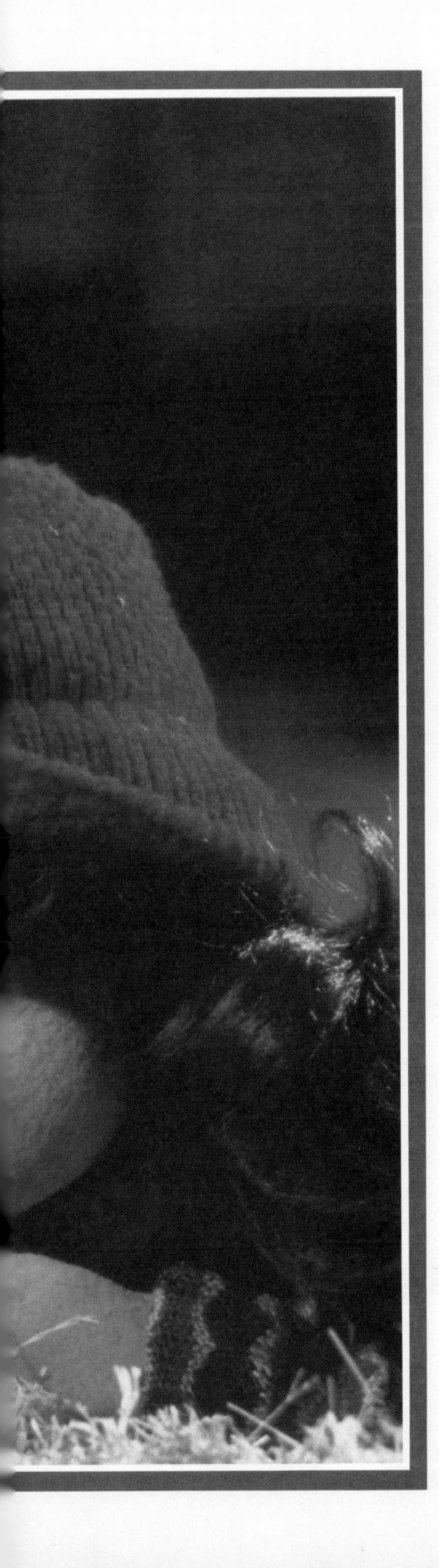

"Well—" said Isaiah slowly. "I think the Professor was a real professor—you know—at a college somewhere. And Mrs. MacTuggle wrote books for kids or something. Then the college ran out of money and closed. And Mrs. M.'s stories got so sad that nobody wanted to buy them anymore. At least I *think* that's what happened."

"But couldn't they get other jobs?" asked Nanny Feather. "How did they end up here?"

"I don't *know,*" said Isaiah impatiently. "I never—well—there are some things you just don't ask other street people about. And they don't ask you."

"I see," said Nanny Feather softly.

"Anyway, here we are. This is the inside of the church."

A light was always left burning in the church itself, and in its soft glow Isaiah saw that the altar guild had already hung pine ropes and holly wreaths for Christmas. Up front, just below the altar, stood a little wooden shed with the Holy Family in it and the shepherds gathered round.

"Wow!" said Nanny Feather. "This is the most beautiful room I ever saw."

"Now you behave yourself," warned Isaiah. "This is God's house."

"Sure." Nanny Feather pointed at the Nativity scene. "Who's that?"

"That's Mary and Joseph with the Christ Child. And the shepherds."

"Never heard of 'em."

"Never heard of 'em?" Isaiah was shocked. "Sure, you have. They're the ones we've been singing about."

"Oh," said Nanny Feather. "*Them.*" She pointed at the figure in the manger. "Which one is He?"

"He's God's *Son,*" Isaiah explained patiently. "The Christ Child. God sent Him to earth that first Christmas to save the world from sin and death."

"That little *Baby?*" Nanny Feather sounded as if she didn't believe him.

"I told you," said Isaiah, "He's God's *Son.* He's—He's like—He's God's Christmas present to the whole world."

"Oh," said Nanny Feather. "Oh. Wow. That was real nice of God."

"Yeah," said Isaiah. "It was. Well, come on. We'd better get back downstairs."

For the next few days they went from street corner to street corner. Each day they collected enough to buy a really good supper. Isaiah could hardly believe how much better those suppers made him feel.

"I wish this could go on forever," he told the others one evening as they finished up a pot of chicken and dumplings. "I wish there were carols for every month of the year."

"I suppose we could try hymns," said Mrs. MacTuggle a little doubtfully.

The Professor shook his head. "It wouldn't work. Folks seem to forget about charity as soon as Christmas is over."

"Wait a minute!" said Isaiah. "The money we get isn't charity. We've *earned* it."

The Professor smiled. "Charity isn't a bad word, Isaiah. It just means love."

"Then people shouldn't forget about it after Christmas," said Nanny Feather. "Not after God's been so nice."

Suddenly Isaiah noticed that she was holding a doll in her lap—a baby doll wrapped up in a blanket. He pointed to it. "Where'd you get that?"

Nanny Feather jumped up so fast that her chair fell over. "A—a nice person gave it to me," she said. "It's a Christmas gift. Don't touch me!"

"Now, now," soothed Mrs. MacTuggle. "No one's going to touch you, child."

"Well, they'd better not." Nanny Feather glared a moment longer. Then she seemed to relax. "I'm going to explore this basement," she announced and drifted off into the shadows, taking her doll with her.

" 'A moody child and wildly wise,' " muttered Isaiah. "Old Emerson was right."

In the days that followed, Nanny Feather spent a lot of time exploring the second basement, and she always took the doll with her. Nothing—not even Gabriel—was as important to her as that doll now, thought Isaiah. Sometimes, late at night when she thought everyone else was asleep, he even heard her talking to it.

Then, almost before anyone realized it, Christmas Eve arrived.

"Guess this is our last day of eating well," said Isaiah, tucking into his pot roast.

"Oh, I think I can manage something for tomorrow too," said Mrs. MacTuggle with a twinkle in her eyes. "And after that, the Lord will provide. He always has, hasn't He?"

Isaiah nodded. "I just wish He'd go on providing pot roast and chicken."

He didn't expect any Christmas presents. They'd never been able to afford them before, and he didn't have anything for anyone else either. But somehow this year Mrs. MacTuggle had managed to knit new woolen mufflers for all of them—even Gabriel.

"Wow!" Nanny Feather wrapped hers clear up to her nose.

"When did you find time to do them?" asked Isaiah.

"Oh, during odd moments when you all were busy." Mrs. MacTuggle laughed. "I'm afraid they're a little *bright.* But I had to use whatever bits of yarn I could find."

"They're perfect," the Professor assured her. "Why, just wearing mine will make me feel more cheerful."

A little later, Nanny Feather disappeared into the shadows as usual and Isaiah and the Professor crept outside. The church folks were having their Christmas Eve service upstairs, so they had to be especially quiet. But as he stood there in the cold air and looked at the stars scattered across the velvet sky, Isaiah felt a deep, warm sort of peace inside him.

" 'If the stars should appear one night in a thousand years, how would we believe and adore!' " said the Professor. "That's Emerson too, Isaiah. Do you understand what he meant?"

Isaiah nodded. "Yes, sir."

Just then someone must have opened a window at the side of the church and they heard voices floating out into the frosty air:

"For Christ is born of Mary,
And gathered all above,
While mortals sleep, the angels keep
Their watch of wond'ring love.
O morning stars, together
Proclaim the holy birth!
And praises sing to God the King,
And peace to all on earth."

"Merry Christmas, Professor," whispered Isaiah.

The Professor squeezed his shoulder. "Merry Christmas, Isaiah."

The next morning Nanny Feather gulped down the hot cereal Mrs. MacTuggle had prepared as a special surprise. Then she dashed off into another part of the basement and returned a moment later carrying a little wooden church building.

"Merry Christmas, everybody," she said, plunking it on the table. "I've got a present for you, too. I found it—right here in the second basement. We're rich!"

Isaiah stared at the little church. *It's awfully old,* he thought. *I can hardly tell what color it used to be. But I can still make out the printing on the roof. M-I-S-S-I-O-N-S. Missions. And right above that is a slot—*

"Well, isn't anyone going to *open* it?" Nanny Feather was jumping up and down with excitement. "It's *full* of money!"

"Calm down, child," said Mrs. MacTuggle. "You'll make yourself sick." But she didn't look any too calm herself. "Hurry up, Professor. Open it!"

Carefully the Professor turned the little church over and pried out a metal disc in the bottom. At once a shower of coins poured onto the table.

Isaiah felt his heart sink. "Coins!" he said in disgust. "It's all just coins, no dollar bills—or even ten-dollar bills."

"You mean we aren't rich after all?" Nanny Feather looked ready to cry.

"Quiet, all of you," ordered the Professor. "I need a better look—"

He rubbed each of the coins with his thumb and then looked at each coin carefully. Some he then put into a separate pile. It took a long time, but at last he dusted off his hands and sat back.

"I don't know a lot about it," he said, "but it seems to me that some of these coins are very old and very valuable—as collectors' items. I'd guess they might even be worth a small fortune."

"Then we *are* rich!" shouted Nanny Feather.

"Great jumping fish feet!" said Isaiah.

Mrs. MacTuggle just threw her apron over her head and sat down.

"But," continued the Professor, "we can't keep them."

"What?" said everyone else.

"We can't keep them," repeated the Professor. "They aren't ours. They belong to the people of the Church of the Good Shepherd. We'll have to turn them over to the minister."

"What rotten luck!" said Isaiah.

"I guess you're right," said Mrs. MacTuggle. "But it does seem hard."

Nanny Feather began to cry. "It was my *Christmas* present to all of you."

The Professor looked sad too. "I guess I should take them up right away," he said. "The minister's probably there now, getting ready for the Christmas Day service."

"But won't he find out—you know—about us?" asked Isaiah.

"I don't know, Isaiah." The Professor sighed. "That's just a chance we'll have to take. I simply can't leave anything as valuable as this might be lying around for someone else to find. I have to deliver it in person."

"Well, I'm going with you," said Isaiah.

"We'll all go," said Mrs. MacTuggle.

"Can we wear our new mufflers?" sniffed Nanny Feather. "Maybe they'll help us feel more cheerful."

"We certainly can," said the Professor.

So, a few moments later, bright mufflers wrapped around their necks, they marched through the front door of the church. Sure enough, the minister was there, arranging some papers on the pulpit. He was an old man with fluffs of white hair behind his ears.

"Good morning," he said pleasantly. "I'm Reverend Merriweather. May I help you?"

"Good morning," said the Professor. "I am Professor John MacTuggle, and these are Mrs. MacTuggle, Isaiah Bond, and Nanny Feather."

"And Gabriel," added Nanny Feather.

"Gabriel?" The Professor's mouth fell open. "Nanny Feather, did you bring that cat into the church?"

"Sure," said Nanny Feather. "He's God's child too, isn't he?"

Reverend Merriweather made a funny noise in his throat.

Is he choking or laughing? wondered Isaiah.

"Never mind," said the minister, coming down from the pulpit. "It's all right. Please go on."

"Well, one of the children found something in your—er—basement," said the Professor. He held out the little church. "I believe some of the coins in it are quite old and valuable. We felt you should have them as soon as possible."

"My sainted Aunt Bessie!" said Reverend Merriweather. He took the church and examined it. "I haven't seen one of these since I was a boy. In fact, I think they date back to my grandfather's day. Children used to put their coins in them for missions. Where did you say you found it?"

"I found it," said Nanny Feather before anyone else could speak. "In the basement under the basement. You know, where we live?"

"Nanny!" cried the other three.

"I—see," said Reverend Merriweather with a strange expression on his face. "Er—why don't we sit down and talk about this?"

"Okay," said Nanny Feather. She perched on the front pew. "It really is a good place to live. Oh, at first I thought it was a dump. But then Isaiah told me how some street people have to sleep under highways and stuff. So now I like it a lot."

Great jumping fish feet! thought Isaiah. *We never warned her! We never told her not to tell anyone about the second basement. She's going to blab the whole thing because she doesn't know any better. I've got to shut her up! Change the subject—or something!*

Desperately he looked around. Then the Nativity scene beneath the altar caught his eye.

"Hey!" he said. "What happened to the Christ Child? It's gone."

"Isn't it terrible?" Reverend Merriweather sighed. "Someone stole it. Can you imagine anyone doing such a thing?"

Nanny Feather jumped up. "Why don't you come see our house?" she asked. "I bet you'd like it."

The Professor stood up too. "Yes," he said in a tired voice. "Please do come, if you have time before the service, that is."

It's like a nightmare, thought Isaiah as he followed the others back to the second basement. *The worst thing I ever imagined is coming true.* He stood at the bottom of the steps as the minister went in and looked around. *I won't cry,* he told himself fiercely. *I won't.*

Then Reverend Merriweather talked to the Professor and Mrs. MacTuggle for a while in a low voice. Isaiah didn't even try to listen. Neither, he noticed, did Nanny Feather. She just sat there on her pew-bed, hugging her doll.

At last Reverend Merriweather came back to the stairs. "Thank you for inviting me into your home," he said. "I must rush up to the service now. But I hope you'll let me come back later."

The Professor bowed his head. "Of course."

"Wait a minute!" yelled Nanny Feather. She ran over to Reverend Merriweather and thrust her doll in his arms. "Here, take your old Christ Child! I thought He was a Christmas present from God to everybody—even me. That's what Isaiah said. But he was wrong. The Christ Child just belongs to the church people. Well, I'm sorry I took Him. So there!"

She burst into tears and ran back into the shadows, just as the old bell in the tower began to ring, calling the faithful to worship.

"My dear God," murmured Reverend Merriweather. He pushed past Isaiah and hurried up the stairs, but not before Isaiah had seen the tears in his eyes.

For a moment everyone was silent. Then Mrs. MacTuggle took charge. "Tea," she said firmly. "That's what we all need—some nice hot tea with plenty of sugar. And you, Isaiah, go find that child. We're going to tell her the story of the first Christmas. And we're going to tell it to her *right.*"

In the end it was the Professor who did the telling and as Isaiah listened to the grand old story again, he felt some of the pain and fear inside him going away.

"But Mary kept all these things, and pondered them in her heart," concluded the Professor and once again Isaiah heard the bell ringing.

Then, suddenly, there was a clatter of footsteps on the stairs and Reverend Merriweather poked his head in. "It's me," he said, "and I've brought some friends. May we come in?"

Again the Professor nodded. "Please do."

Why, he must have brought the whole church! thought Isaiah as people poured down the stairs. Somehow they all found a place to sit or stand or lean. Then Reverend Merriweather went up to the Professor and handed him the little wooden church.

"We want you to have it," he said simply. "We think there is enough in there to buy you a little house somewhere."

"Glory be!" said Mrs. MacTuggle. "Then the children can go to school."

"We have people who can help you find jobs too," said Reverend Merriweather. "And a lawyer who can help you keep the children for good." He paused and again Isaiah saw tears in his eyes. "Please let us do this," he said. "You will be giving us so much."

The Professor looked down. "I don't know," he said slowly. "It's charity, pure and simple. I don't know if we can—"

"Wait a minute!" interrupted Isaiah. "What's wrong with charity? You said yourself that it just means love."

"He's right," said Reverend Merriweather. "That's what we want to give you—love. And we want you to love us too, to be part of us here at the Church of the Good Shepherd—upstairs."

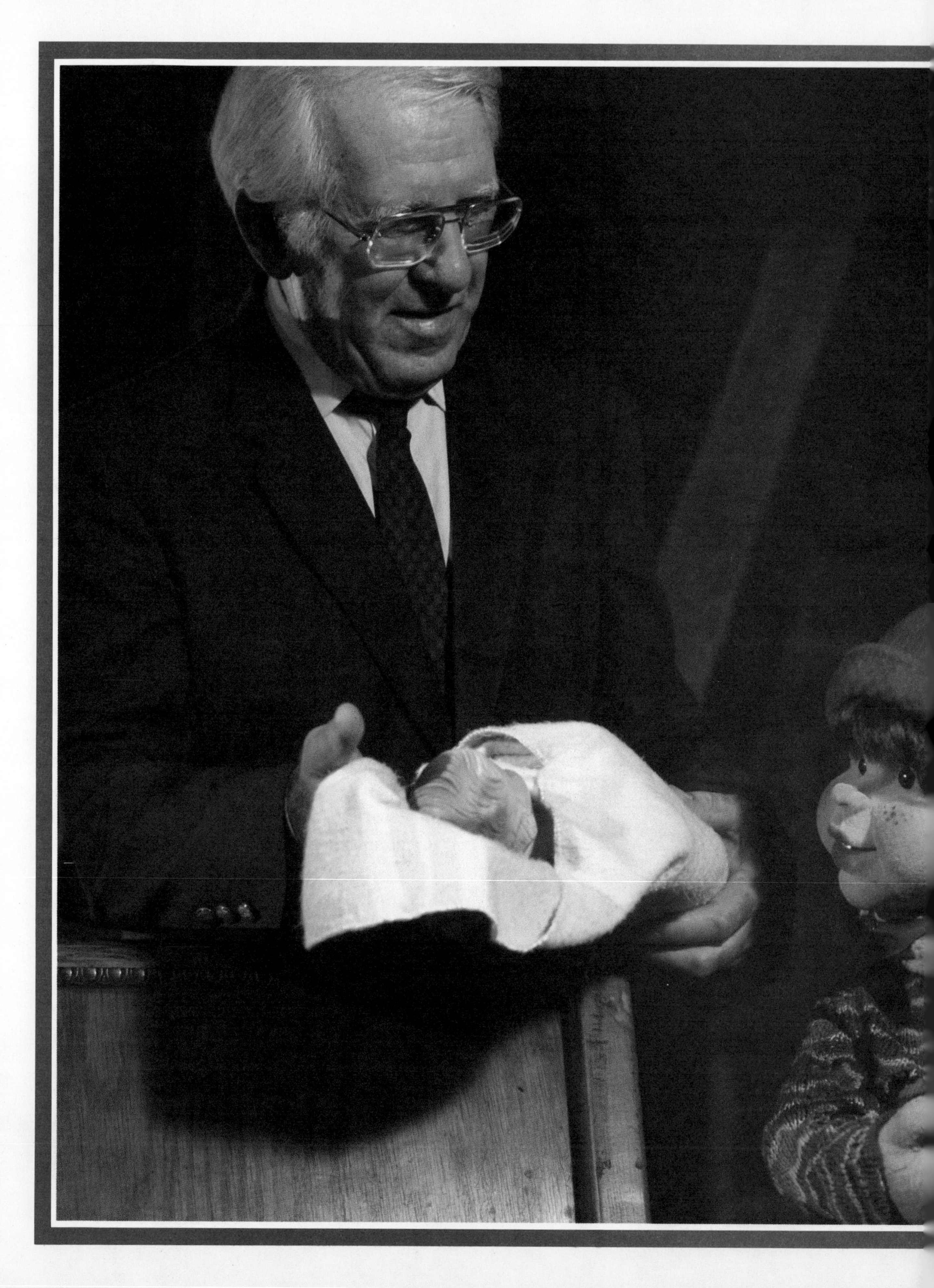

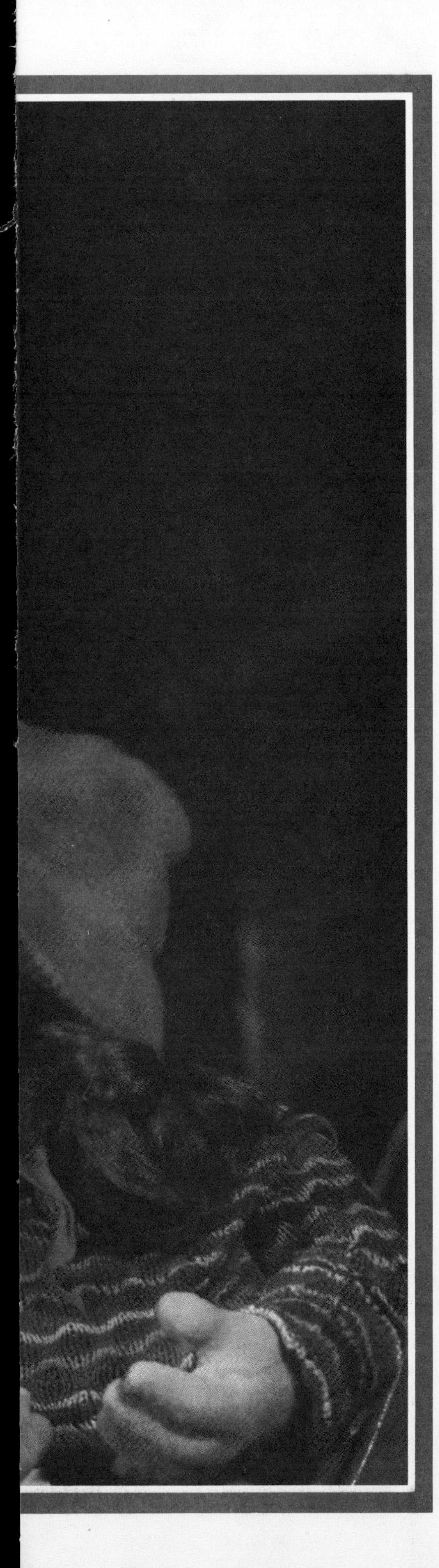

He took a bundle from a woman beside him and gave it to Nanny Feather. "It's the Christ Child," he said. "God's gift of love. We want you to keep Him."

The Professor smiled then. "All right," he said. "We will accept your love. And thank you."

"Thank you! Thank you!" yelled Nanny Feather. Then, like a thunderbolt, she was in the Professor's arms—along with the Christ Child and Gabriel.

"Glory be!" cried Mrs. MacTuggle. "We can touch her! She won't break anymore!" And she threw her apron over her head and sat down.

Isaiah didn't say anything. He was too full of joy for saying. There was only one way he could let all of that joy out. So he threw back his head and started to sing.

"Where children pure and happy
Pray to the blessèd Child,
Where misery cries out to Thee,
Son of the mother mild—"

Then, softly, everyone in the second basement joined in as, far above, the old bell rang.

"Where charity stands watching
And faith holds wide the door,
The dark night wakes, the glory breaks,
And Christmas comes once more."

Ages 2½ To